THE DISTANCE BETWEEN STARS

THE DISTANCE BETWEEN STARS

Written by

ULLAS N

For everyone who has ever loved quietly,

from a careful distance,

and been changed by it.

"The most painful thing is losing yourself in the process of loving someone too much, and forgetting that you are special too."

Ernest Hemingway

PART ONE

Radiant

Chapter One

The Beginning of Everything

September First Year

September arrived the way it always did at the start of something new on a Wednesday, in the middle of the week, as though time itself didn't bother with grand entrances. The sky above Ashfield University was the particular shade of blue that belongs only to early autumn, the kind that seems too good to last, and it was warm in the way that warmth in September always feels borrowed pleasant but aware of itself, knowing that November is not far behind.

Oliver Hayes arrived the night before. He did this deliberately. He had researched the orientation schedule, established that most students would arrive on the morning of the first day, and made the calculation that arriving the evening before would give him twelve hours to learn the geography of his new environment before it filled up with other people. This was not antisocial. It was, he had explained to his mother when she had questioned the logic, simply efficient.

"You could make friends on the journey," his mother Margaret had said, standing in the doorway of his childhood bedroom watching him pack with a precision that still surprised her after eighteen years.

“I could,” Oliver had agreed, folding a grey jumper with the kind of attention most people reserve for important documents. “Or I could arrive with a clear picture of the campus layout and spend that energy on things I’m less prepared for.”

Margaret had looked at her son for a long moment the careful, observant look she’d been giving him since he was old enough to choose his own seat at the dinner table, always the same chair, always facing the window and she had said, quietly, “Just don’t spend so much time preparing that you forget to arrive, love.”

He had thought about that on the train, watching the city dissolve into countryside. He had thought about it again as he unpacked his books in his new room a single, third floor, window overlooking the main courtyard and arranged them alphabetically by author and then reconsidered and arranged them by the order he intended to read them, which took forty minutes and felt more honest. He had thought about it one more time as he lay on his new narrow bed in the dark, listening to the sounds of an empty building, and tried to imagine what tomorrow would feel like.

He couldn’t. He was good at imagining most things, but not this the sensation of walking into a room full of people who didn’t know him yet. That required information he didn’t have. He would have to wait and see.

He was, in this as in many things, patient.

The orientation hall was a large, wood-panelled room with high windows on the south side and a slightly uneven floor that caught the light at odd angles. It smelled of cleaning products and a faint undertow of old paper the institutional smell of places that have housed generations of young people all passing through, all certain that what they were about to begin was significant, most of them right about that in ways they wouldn't understand until much later.

Oliver sat in the third row. This was a calculation as deliberate as all his calculations. The front row carried the weight of expectation the ones who sat there were assumed to be enthusiastic, or trying to appear so, and Oliver was neither. The back row announced a particular kind of disengagement that he also didn't feel. The third row was a careful, calibrated neutral, a position from which you could observe without being observed, where you could hear everything without being required to contribute, where the most interesting things usually happened.

He had his notebook open on the desk. His pen was uncapped. These were the two items of social armour he had brought to his first day of university: a notebook and an uncapped pen.

He was tracing a small knot in the wood grain of his desk with one finger when the hall began to fill.

He heard: the particular pitch of nervous laughter higher than relaxed laughter, more frequent, serving a social purpose distinct from amusement. He heard: the scrape of chairs, the rustle of bags, the comparative quietness of the students who, like him, had not yet found their role in this new world and were waiting to be assigned one. He heard: a group near the door who were already in the process of becoming friends.

And then, from somewhere to his left and several rows behind him, he heard her laugh.

He did not know, in that moment, that he would spend the next year thinking about that sound. He only knew, in the moment, that it was different from the other sounds in the room. Not louder. Not more musical. Not exceptional in any way he could have articulated. Only genuine.

He looked up.

She came through the door with three other girls. She was speaking with her hands, which Oliver noticed immediately because it was unusual most people held their hands still when they talked. She held nothing back. Her arms described arcs in the air that matched the shape of her sentences, and her dark hair was tucked behind one ear but kept escaping on the other side, and she was wearing a yellow cardigan over a darker shirt, and she was laughing with all of her face, with no reservation at all.

She sat down two rows behind him and to the left, which meant he could not see her without turning around. He did not turn around.

The orientation began. A dean spoke. A student representative spoke. Slides were shown. Oliver wrote things in his notebook in his usual careful handwriting, and he was genuinely interested in some of it, and he would have told you that his attention was entirely on the information being presented. This would not have been entirely true.

He was also, in the background of his careful attention, cataloguing the laugh he had heard. Filing it somewhere. Understanding, slowly, that it had changed something in the room's atmosphere for him not dramatically, nothing so clear or legible as drama but in the quiet, specific way that a window opening changes the quality of air in a room.

He did not look for her name on the list. He did not ask who she was. He went back to his room that evening, made himself tea with the small kettle he'd brought from home, arranged his desk lamp for optimal reading light, and read for two hours before sleeping.

But before he slept, he thought, briefly, involuntarily: I wonder what her name is.

He did not think it was the beginning of anything. He wouldn't know that for some time yet.

Chapter Two

Learning Her Without Speaking

October First Year

The beautiful thing about October and Oliver was someone who noticed beautiful things, even when he didn't quite know what to do with them was the way it made everything visible by stripping it back. The trees gave up their leaves and revealed their shapes. The long days shortened and the light became angled, thoughtful, casting long shadows where summer had cast none. October was the month of clarity. Of honest assessment. Of seeing things as they were rather than as they seemed.

Oliver learned things about Amelia Clark he had learned her name from the class list; he had written it in the inside cover of his notebook; he had not examined too carefully what this meant the way he learned most things he cared about. Through patient observation. Through the accumulation of small facts.

He learned that she arrived to Professor Harmon's English Literature lecture four minutes before the start, which was different from the people who arrived on time (efficient) and from the people who arrived early (anxious) and from the people who arrived late (either disorganised or performing cool). Four minutes was its own category. Four minutes was the margin of someone who was relaxed about most things but not careless about them.

He learned that she spent those four minutes talking to whoever happened to be near. Not seeking people out she wasn't aggressive about it, not predatory in her sociability she simply responded to proximity. If you were within conversational range of Amelia Clark, you became, briefly, part of her world.

He learned that she preferred window seats. This was not unusual many people preferred window seats but the particular way she claimed them was: not hurriedly, not possessively, but with the quiet certainty of someone who knows what they want and trusts that the world will provide it.

He learned that she bit her lower lip when she was thinking. Not constantly only in certain moments, when a question had been posed that genuinely required thought. It was, he thought, the only moment when Amelia Clark looked entirely unguarded.

He learned about the succulent on a Thursday in the third week of October. She had reached into her bag for her notebook and the small terracotta pot had come with it attached to nothing, simply present in the bag because she carried it with her, apparently and she had set it on the desk beside her notebook with the matter-of-fact air of someone for whom this was entirely normal. A tiny, spiky-leafed succulent in a pot the size of a fist, slightly dusty, clearly old, clearly tended.

She had glanced at it, adjusted its position slightly so that it faced more fully toward the window, and then returned to her notes as though nothing unusual had happened.

Oliver had looked at the succulent for a long time.

He wondered who had given it to her, or whether she had chosen it herself, which seemed more likely she struck him as someone who chose her own things. He wondered whether she talked to it, which also seemed likely. He wondered how long she had carried it.

He catalogued her laughter styles there were four, as best he could tell.

The surprised laugh: short, involuntary, the kind that escapes before it can be contained. This was the rarest and the truest. It was the laugh that came from the orientation hall that first day, the one that had split the air and changed something in him.

The delighted laugh: longer, with her head tilted back slightly, often with her hand raised toward her face.

The social laugh: warm but measured, the sound she made when courtesy required an expression of amusement she didn't entirely feel. Not false she was not a false person but diplomatic.

And the quiet laugh: the rarest one of all. The one that was almost only breath. He had only heard it once, and something about the privacy of it the fact that it seemed aimed at no one, that it was simply felt and released had stayed with him.

He was building a picture. He understood this, even then. He wasn't stalking her. He wasn't obsessing in any way that felt dangerous or desperate. He was simply paying very close attention. To something that mattered.

Chapter Three

Almost

November First Year

November arrived with the conviction of a season that knows it's right. The warmth of October gave up. The sky lowered. The leaves finally let go, and the campus paths became carpeted in gold and brown. Oliver wore a coat now grey wool, bought three years ago and cared for accordingly and he walked to class with his hands in his pockets and his shoulders slightly hunched, which was not against the cold so much as it was simply how he moved through the world.

November was the month he almost talked to her.

The campus coffee shop was a problem on Thursday afternoons. Between three and six it became what Oliver privately thought of as maximally social full to the point where conversation was necessary rather than optional. He had learned this in the second week of term and had adjusted accordingly.

He went to the coffee shop on Thursdays at two. He always got the small table near the back, and he drank a flat white and read for an hour and then, usually, felt adequately restored to continue the afternoon.

He was on page forty-seven of a novel about a lighthouse keeper when the door opened.

He knew before he looked up. He couldn't have explained how, except that he had become, without meaning to, attuned to her in the way that certain presences become legible before they announce themselves.

She was alone. Her cheeks were flushed with cold. She was unwinding a striped scarf from her neck as she crossed to the counter, and she had a large bag over one shoulder and a book tucked under her arm, and she was scanning the room as she moved.

He looked at his book. He read the same sentence four times. He retained nothing.

She got her drink. She turned from the counter and surveyed the room and then because the universe was operating on some principle that Oliver could not have named the strap of her bag caught on the back of a chair as she passed it, and she lurched slightly, and their eyes met for a single, clear, unambiguous moment.

She had brown eyes. He had known this, had observed this, but this was different a direct line of attention from her to him, which had not happened before.

"Hi," she said. Easy. Not surprised to be speaking to him.

He said: "Hi."

She smiled the social smile, the warm-but-measured one and moved to her table.

He went back to his book. He read the sentence for the sixth time. He still retained nothing.

He left twenty minutes before he had intended to. He walked around the campus for a while, hands in his pockets, in the November afternoon with its cold and its bare branches. He thought about a pair of brown eyes and the word hi and the question of whether that had been an experience or simply an event.

He decided it was both. He walked back to his room. He made tea. He did not sleep particularly well that night, but he attributed this to the coffee.

He was eighteen and not yet very good at lying to himself. He would get better.

Chapter Four

The Party

December First Year

The invitation arrived in the group message for the English programme in the first week of December. Not personal. Not curated. Everyone in the programme was welcome, which meant there was no reasonable basis for declining.

Oliver spent three days constructing one.

He didn't go to parties. This was not a statement of moral principle or social anxiety in any clinical sense it was simply that parties optimised for a kind of spontaneous social interaction that he had never found natural. He had a rule about them. The rule was: no.

He told himself, on Thursday, that he wasn't going. On Saturday he spent forty minutes in front of his bathroom mirror arguing with his hair and admitted to himself at last what he had known since the invitation arrived: he was going because she would be there.

Not because of any plan. Not with any expectation. He was going because there was a small, quiet part of him that was tired of the distance, and because

December was a month that did something to careful people that made them less careful.

He went.

The house was loud and warm in the way of occupied spaces on cold nights. Someone had strung lights. The kitchen was where most people were, as kitchens at parties always tend to be.

She was in the kitchen.

Of course she was. Amelia Clark existed at the centre of things, not by design but by gravity. She was wearing something green and she was laughing and she had a glass of something in one hand and she was leaning forward slightly as she listened to someone, which was the way she listened all of her tilted toward whoever was speaking.

Oliver stood in the doorway for a moment. Then he moved to the edge of the room, where the wall was, and he found a position that was defensible not too close to the crowd, not so far as to look deliberately removed and he got a drink he didn't particularly want and held it because the holding gave his hands something to do.

He watched her the way you watch something that gives off warmth. Not greedily. Not desperately. With the quality of attention you give to a fire when you are cold drawn to it, standing at its edge, not quite certain whether you're allowed to come closer.

Then someone changed the music. The density of the crowd redistributed. And in the space created by this redistribution, Amelia Clark moved slightly closer to him.

She turned. And he was there.

"Hey," she said. "You're in my English Lit class, right? Oliver?"

The use of his name did something to him that he would spend a long time trying to describe and never quite manage. It was as though the word had weight as though hearing his name in her voice gave it a substance it hadn't possessed before.

"Yeah," he said. And then something loosened. Some carefully maintained guard gave way, not dramatically, not loudly, but in the manner of a door that has been locked for a long time and opens when you press it at the right angle. He said:

"You, um. You were holding a book in the library once. Pressed it against your chest."

The words existed in the air. He became immediately aware that he had said them. He became aware, a half-second later, that they were strange specific in the way that implies attention.

Amelia blinked. Then she laughed the surprised one, the rare one, the genuine one.

"Oh my God, that's so specific," she said. "Which book was it?"

"I don't know. I couldn't see the cover."

She laughed again. "It was The God of Small Things. I'd been looking for it for months." She tilted her head. "You noticed that?"

"I notice things," he said.

She looked at him. For a real moment. In that look, Oliver felt something he had not expected to feel in a crowded kitchen in December, something that would take him several years to understand: the specific sensation of being seen by someone who sees people well.

"I believe you," she said.

Three words. Small words. Words that meant nothing in particular, that anyone might have said, that required nothing and implied nothing. Except that they landed in him like something dropped into still water.

Someone called her name from across the room. She glanced toward the sound, then back at Oliver. She smiled the warmer version and said, "See you in class, Oliver."

And she was gone, drawn back into the bright centre of things, and Oliver stood by the wall with his untouched drink and three words in his chest that he would carry for the rest of the year.

I believe you.

He carried them carefully. He carried them home.

Chapter Five

The Last Piece

April End of First Year

The last day of the first year arrived in the way of all last days suddenly, and then all at once, and then with the strange simultaneity of an ending that you knew was coming and that managed to be surprising anyway.

Oliver had packed his room into two bags and a box. He had cleaned carefully not compulsively, but with the respect you give to a space you have inhabited through something important. He had several hours before his ride.

He went for a walk.

He did not plan to go to the English building courtyard. He ended up there anyway, which was either coincidence or the unconscious direction of his feet toward the place that had been most meaningful this year.

The courtyard was warm in the April sun the first genuinely warm day since March. The stone bench was there. The scraggly tree at the edge had finally gone green, pale and new and committed to its greenness in the tentative way of things that have recently decided to be alive.

Oliver sat down. He put his face up to the sun. He closed his eyes.

He had been sitting there for perhaps ten minutes when he heard her.

Not the laugh. Just her voice talking to someone, a conversation he couldn't quite hear at the level of words, only at the level of tone. She was saying something and then the other voice replied and then she said, clearly: "I know, I know. Same time next year," and then the sound of her laughing, warm and easy, already somewhere else even while she was still here.

He kept his eyes closed. He heard her footsteps unhurried, crossing the courtyard and he heard them recede, and then diminish, and then disappear into the ordinary sounds of the campus.

He sat there for a while longer. He thought about a yellow cardigan in September. He thought about a laugh that had split the air of an orientation hall and changed something in him without knowing it. He thought about a book pressed to a chest and a mouth that said his name. He thought about "I believe you."

He thought: I loved you from far away, and it was enough to change me.

He thought: You were kind to a stranger, and the stranger was me, and I'll carry that.

He stood up. He picked up his jacket. He walked back toward the dormitory.

It didn’t feel like sadness. It felt like something that had mattered.

Epilogue: First Year

The Letter He Never Sent

That evening, before he carried his bags down to the car, he sat at his desk for the last time and opened his journal.

He had kept journals since he was fourteen. Not diaries he was precise about the distinction. Diaries recorded events. Journals recorded thought. He had never used a journal to say anything to anyone. That was not what they were for.

But he opened it, and he took his pen, and he began:

Dear Amelia,

You don't know me very well. I know you know my name, because you said it once at a party in December and it is one of my favourite sounds now, which I recognise is a strange thing to say about a sound you didn't even know you were making.

I've sat near you all year. I've watched you make friends with strangers the way other people breathe effortlessly, without apparent effort. I've watched you hold a book like it was something precious. I've watched you laugh like you meant it.

I never talked to you. I want you to know that this was not because of you. You would have talked back. The wall was mine. It has always been mine.

But here is what I want to say: knowing you even from a distance, even in this sideways, one-sided, nearly-invisible way made me better at being me. You reminded me that the world has warm things in it.

I hope someone in your life loves you the way you deserve loudly, and clearly, and without the distance I have always kept.

I hope you keep holding books against your chest.

Oliver

He closed the journal. He sat for a moment in the quiet of the room he had inhabited for nine months, now empty of himself except for what could not be packed.

He picked up his bags. He turned off the lamp. He went downstairs and out into the April evening where his ride was waiting and the campus was golden and he carried her name all the way home.

Some loves live entirely in the chest of one person. Quiet and unconfirmed, and no less real for it.

PART TWO

The Years After

Chapter Six

The World Without Her In It

Summer After First Year   Ashford

Oliver went home to Ashford the way a tide goes out from shore quietly, without announcement, leaving the sand exactly as it found it. The train took four hours, and he spent most of them watching the countryside resolve from city grey into something greener, something that breathed differently.

His mother was waiting at the station with a yellow umbrella even though the sky was entirely clear. She always brought the umbrella. She had told him once that weather was a thing you prepared for, not reacted to, and Oliver had grown up understanding this as a metaphor for how Margaret Hayes moved through the world: armoured against surprises, warmly, without alarm.

"You look thin," she said, and she pulled him into a hug that smelled of lavender and the particular soap she had used his entire life.

"I ate," he said.

"I didn't say you didn't. I said you look thin. Those are different statements."

His father Robert was waiting in the car. Robert Hayes was a compact man with grey at his temples and large hands that had spent thirty years bending the world into right angles. He clapped Oliver on the shoulder when Oliver got in and said, "Good," which Oliver had spent eighteen years learning to translate. Good meant: I missed you. I'm glad you're back. I love you in the way I know how to love you.

The house smelled the same. Oliver had forgotten how much he had been counting on this.

* * *

Jack Fernandez arrived the next afternoon, which was both uninvited and utterly predictable. He knocked three times fast always three times fast, always the same knock, the same since they were twelve years old.

"Mate," Jack said, lowering himself into the armchair in Oliver's room. "Good year?"

"Educational."

"That's what it's for." A pause. "Was there a girl?"

Oliver looked at the ceiling.

"There's always a girl," Jack said. "What's her name?"

"Amelia."

"Amelia." Jack said it the way he said all names he was encountering for the first time as though trying it on, assessing its weight. "What's the damage?"

"She doesn't know I exist." He corrected himself. "Knew. Didn't. Past tense."

Later, Daniel Okafor came over, because that was how it worked with the three of them one arrived and the others followed by some unspoken law of their particular gravity. Daniel was quieter than Jack and more intuitive than Oliver; he had the gift of understanding things without being told them.

He brought food from his mother's kitchen rice and stew and a container of fried plantains that were already warm from the journey. It was a form of clairvoyance disguised as hospitality.

Later, when Jack had gone and Daniel was pulling on his jacket at the door, Daniel said, without looking up: "You all right? Really?"

"I will be," Oliver said.

Daniel nodded. "Good enough. For now, that's good enough."

Chapter Seven

Second Year, New Distances

September Second Year

He saw her the first week of second year. She was crossing the campus green with Priya and another girl, all three of them laughing. She looked, from a distance, exactly as he had remembered her looking. Which was either the most ordinary thing in the world or the opposite.

He was walking in the other direction. She looked up at exactly the moment when a slightly more careful universe would have looked away. Their eyes met.

"Hey!" she said. Genuinely surprised, and genuinely warm.

"Hey," he said.

She smiled the real one and kept walking. He kept walking. Six words between them, and then twenty feet, and then she was past him and he was past her and the campus continued in both directions.

She remembered him. It was, he thought, possibly the most dangerous thing that had happened to him in nineteen years.

Second year arranged itself differently. They had a Thursday morning seminar together seventeen students, Professor Harmon at the front, a table in a horseshoe shape that made it impossible to avoid looking at people. Amelia sat three seats to his left.

She argued with Professor Harmon in the second seminar. This was the first time Oliver had seen her in the context of genuine intellectual engagement rather than social ease, and the distinction was interesting she was less fluid when she was arguing, less immediately graceful, but more alive in a different way.

After the third seminar, she turned to him. "What did you think of his point about unreliable narrators?" she asked. Directly. As though she had been thinking about his opinion for some time and had finally decided to ask it.

"I think Harmon's right that readers tend to distrust unreliable narrators," he said slowly, choosing each word with the care he always gave to words. "But I think that distrust is actually where the interesting reading happens. The places where you can't be certain what's true that's not a flaw in the text. It's the text's most honest moment."

Amelia looked at him for a moment with an expression he couldn't fully read. Then she opened her red notebook and wrote something.

"What did you write?" he asked, and surprised himself by asking it.

She tilted the notebook toward him.

She had written: The distrust is where the reading happens. Oliver H.

"I attribute my quotes," she said. "It's a habit. If something is worth writing down, it's worth saying where it came from."

He didn't know what to say to this. He said: "Thank you."

He watched her go, and thought about his name written in her red notebook in her handwriting, and felt the very specific, very quiet sensation of being simultaneously more real and more invisible than he had ever been.

* * *

They became something. The word for it didn't exist quite, or the available words were both too large and too small. They were not friends in the full sense of the word. They were not acquaintances. They were people who talked after seminar, who ended up at the same coffee shop and nodded across rooms, who began texting first about the reading, then about adjacent things, then by November about nothing at all which is to say about everything.

Amelia texted the way she talked: with her whole self and no particular economy. Long messages that followed their own internal logic; short messages that were just a sentence or an image she had found funny; voice notes at eleven pm that began "okay so I was thinking about what Harmon said."

Oliver texted the way he did everything: carefully. He read what he had written before he sent it. He was always a little behind himself when it came to her.

"You take forever to reply," she told him once during a study session in the library.

"I think about what I'm saying before I say it."

"That's either very admirable or extremely inconvenient. I haven't decided."

"It's probably both."

She laughed the surprised one, the genuine one and he filed it away. He understood what was happening to him with complete clarity and zero ability to do anything useful about it.

Chapter Eight

The Year of Almost Saying It

Third Year December

There was a night in December of third year that Oliver would think about for a long time. They were in the library he had been there since seven, she had arrived at nine and it was past ten, and the library had taken on the quality it had late at night: quieter, warmer, more like a ship than a building, sailing through the dark with its few remaining passengers.

Amelia came and sat across from him. She had been on the far side of the library for the past hour, and she migrated now with the naturalness of someone who has decided something without deciding it simply felt the pull of a familiar presence and followed it.

She put her chin in her hand and looked at him. "Tell me something," she said.

"Something about what?"

"Anything. I have been staring at the same paragraph for an hour. I need a different sentence."

Oliver said: "Did you know that certain species of jellyfish are technically biologically immortal? When they're stressed, they revert to their juvenile state and begin the cycle again."

Amelia blinked. A beat. Then: "That is the most Oliver thing I have ever heard."

"You asked for something."

"Do you think it sounds like a good deal? Starting over every time things get hard?"

"I think it sounds lonely," he said eventually. "Being new every time. Never carrying anything forward. Never knowing what you've accumulated."

She went quiet. It was the particular quiet she went into when she was thinking rather than processing. She was looking at him differently now.

"You're going to be important to someone," she said. Not coyly, not romantically. Simply as a fact. The way you state the colour of the sky.

Oliver felt it land in the centre of him and stay.

"What made you say that?"

"The way you think about things," she said, returning to her notebook. "The way you take everything seriously. The way you never say anything you haven't actually thought about." A pause. "Those are rare things."

He stayed for another hour. He did not write another word of notes in any colour.

* * *

He almost said it in February.

She had mentioned a film Italian, subtitled and she had said, in a way that could have been general, "Someone should come with me," and he had said, before he had time to process the saying of it, "I'll come."

Priya cancelled. Chloe had another commitment. It was just the two of them, in a darkened cinema on a Saturday night, watching something beautiful and devastating about Italy in the 1950s.

Afterward, walking back, she was talking about the film with the energy of someone who has been keeping a feeling in while sitting politely in public. He listened. The cold was real she had pulled her coat tight and she walked slightly closer to him than she might have otherwise.

At the corner where their routes diverged, she stopped. "I had a really good time," she said. And she looked at him when she said it not at her phone, not at the street at him.

He said: "Me too."

He thought: I have been in love with you since September of first year, since the moment your laugh split the air of that orientation hall. I have been in love with you through seminars and coffee shops and a year of texts and a photograph of a judgemental cloud and this walk home in the cold.

He said: "Same time next week, if you want. There's a Kurosawa retrospective."

"I want," she said. And went.

Oliver stood at the corner for a moment. He put his hands in his pockets. He walked home and texted Jack: I should have said something.

Jack, who was always awake: Said what?

Oliver put his phone down and didn't reply. Jack, who knew the shape of certain silences, didn't ask again.

Chapter Nine

The Last Year of That Life

Fourth Year Ending

Final year arrived with the weight particular to endings the consciousness of finitude that falls on everything in that last year like a different quality of light, making familiar things simultaneously more vivid and more precious.

Oliver applied for positions at three consulting firms. He received two offers. He chose the smaller firm Meridian Consulting, based in the city because it had room to grow in the particular way he understood growing: not quickly, not ostentatiously, but deep.

Amelia was applying for journalism. She had the quality, he had noticed, of being wanted by industries that deal in human connection.

"Everyone has an opinion about which one I should take," she told him one afternoon, wrapping both hands around her coffee cup. "Chloe thinks the one that pays most. Priya thinks the one with the best stories. My mum thinks the one closest to home."

"What do you think?"

"I think I want to go somewhere new. Somewhere that isn't anywhere I've already been."

"Then go somewhere new," he said.

* * *

They graduated in June. The ceremony was long and formal and moving in the specific way of ceremonies that contain a genuine threshold.

Amelia found him just before he left. She stepped out from her group and walked over with the directness she had for people she actually intended to speak to.

"I got the job," she said. "The journalism one. Westport."

He felt something that was complicated and simultaneous genuine happiness for her, and the particular ache of a door he had not opened slowly closing. "Priya's choice," he said.

"She's completely insufferable about it." She glanced back at her group, then at him. "I'll miss our Thursdays."

She hugged him. Longer. More deliberate. As though she were also doing the accounting that he was doing.

"Stay in touch," she said, pulling back.

"I will."

She went back to her group. He watched her go. That's it, he thought. That was it.

He was wrong about this. But he wouldn't know that for some time yet.

PART THREE

The Long Quiet

Chapter Ten

The City, The Work, The Finding

Two Years After Graduation

The city received Oliver the way it received everyone indifferently, enormously, with an absolute absence of ceremony that was somehow clarifying. Nobody knew him here. Nobody had expectations of him here.

He found a flat on the east side, third floor, with a window that looked over a small courtyard where someone had planted a lilac tree that would bloom, he was told by his neighbour, every May. He furnished it slowly, with the care he gave to things that would be lived with: a good reading chair by the window. A desk that was the right height. Bookshelves he built himself from timber and brackets.

Meridian Consulting was demanding in the way of good work: it stretched him. His manager, Patricia Devlin, told him after his first six months: "You think like the building, not the room. Most people can only see the room they're in. You see the load-bearing structure."

He worked long hours. He read. He had dinner with Jack on Thursday nights, a habit that had organised itself without either of them designing it. He went on occasional dates, arranged by Jack with the persistent optimism of a person who fundamentally believes that connection is possible if you simply create enough situations in which it might occur. He was pleasant company. He asked good questions. He listened carefully. But there was always, beneath the pleasantness, a certain absence.

In all visible ways, he was fine.

* * *

He found her on a Tuesday in October. He was scrolling through professional networks, and the algorithm offered him something he hadn't searched for: her face, slightly out of focus, laughing at an outdoor event, exactly right, exactly her. Amelia Clark. Journalist. Westport.

He sat with his phone for a while. He thought: don't. He thought: she said stay in touch. He typed: Hey. It's Oliver Hayes, from uni. Hope Westport is treating you well.

Twenty minutes later his phone buzzed.

Oliver Hayes! I was literally thinking about you last week when I found something I'd written in my old notebook 'the distrust is where the reading happens'. With your name next to it. That quote has lived rent-free in my head for two years. How are you? What city are you in??

He read it twice. He smiled. It was a small smile, private, somewhat helpless. She kept the quote. She had written it in her notebook two years ago and she still has the notebook.

He wrote back. They fell back into each other the way familiar things do easily, then deeply, then with a naturalness that made the intervening years feel like a pause rather than a gap.

December came. Her birthday was the fourteenth. He had known what he was going to do before he admitted it to himself.

He found an independent bookshop that did gift delivery. He spent an evening choosing: a collection of essays by a journalist she had mentioned admiring. A novel with a blue cover that he had read and believed she would love. A small illustrated book about the ocean. He wrote a card. He crossed out what he wrote. He wrote it again. He left the return address blank.

She called him on the fifteenth. "I got the most mysterious package," she said, and he could hear the smile in it.

"Oh?"

"Three books. No return address. The card just said Happy Birthday Amelia. Oliver, I have been wanting that essay collection for months. Someone out there knows my taste extremely well."

"Secret admirer," he said.

"Apparently." A pause that held something he couldn't name. "It wasn't you, was it?"

His heartbeat did something complicated. "Why would it be me?"

"I don't know. You know my taste."

"So does the internet's algorithm."

"True." She moved on. "Happy birthday to me, anyway. Now tell me about your week."

He told her about his week. He sat in his chair with his courtyard and his lilac tree bare outside, and he listened to her voice across the distance, and felt the familiar specific weight of carrying something too heavy for one person and not knowing how to set it down.

Chapter Eleven

The Natural Drift

Year Three After Graduation

It happened gradually. All drifts happen gradually not in a single moment but in accumulated small distances. He noticed when it started, the way you notice when a sound you have gotten used to begins to diminish.

A reply that took a day instead of hours. A call that wasn't returned and was replaced with a brief text. A week where they didn't speak, and then a second week, and then quietly, without announcement a month.

He understood. She was in motion, always in motion, and the people and things she collected were numerous and all demanding. She was not being unkind. She was being herself.

"She's pulling back," Jack said. They were at dinner Thursday, Jack's parents' restaurant.

"She's busy," Oliver said.

"She's always been busy. Busy people make time for the things that matter to them." Jack put his fork down. "Have you told her? Any of it?"

"No."

"Then she doesn't know what she's pulling back from. She thinks she's being a bit rubbish at texting. She doesn't know she's leaving you behind."

"If you tell her," Jack said, more gently, "at least you know. One way or another."

"And if she doesn't feel the same?"

"Then you grieve it properly. Not like this not in this half-alive way you're doing it in currently. This isn't patience, Ollie. You're standing still and calling it patience."

"Maybe patience is what I have," he said.

Jack picked up his fork. He said "Sure," in the voice he reserved for moments when he disagreed and had decided not to fight. Oliver knew what that voice meant. He didn't argue with it.

* * *

December came again. Her birthday came again. He sent a package. Same anonymity, same care. A small watercolour set with quality brushes. A small potted succulent in a hand-thrown ceramic pot. A card that said only: For the person who makes every room worth being in.

She texted him three days later. "My mystery benefactor has struck again. Whoever they are, they have been paying extremely close attention."

"Do you have suspects?"

"Chloe thinks it's a secret ex. Priya thinks it's someone at work." A pause. "What do you think?"

"I think it sounds like someone who cares about you in a very particular way."

"A very quiet way," she said. "I think it's someone who's quiet about the things that matter most to them." Another pause. "I hope I get to thank them someday."

Oliver typed and deleted three different responses. He settled on: Sounds like you're loved.

She replied: I really think I am. It's a strange feeling.

Strange. He held that word. He thought: that's the thing about being loved from a distance it's always slightly strange, because you can feel the warmth of it without knowing its source.

Chapter Twelve

The Quiet Years of Building

Three to Four Years After Graduation

He built things during those years. That was what happened to all the contained energy, all the feeling with no place to go it went sideways, into work, into the slow careful assembly of something that would last.

The consultancy idea arrived the way Oliver's best ideas always arrived: not dramatically, not in a single moment of inspiration, but as a slow recognition. He saw a gap. He knew how to fill it.

He told Jack first. They were in Jack's car, stopped at a red light. Oliver said, without preamble: "I think I want to start a company."

The light changed. Jack drove. He said, after twenty seconds of processing: "Tell me more."

When Oliver finished, Jack said: "I'm in."

"I didn't ask you."

"I know. But you should have. You don't have front-facing energy. I do. You have the thinking. I have the selling. Daniel knows every creative contact in the city."

They called it Helix Solutions. Jack's name, Daniel's typography for the logo a helix in dark blue. They operated out of borrowed office space for the first six months, then a small real office that smelled of fresh paint and possibility.

He sent a birthday package every year. Without fail. Without announcement. Without return address.

Year three: a first edition of short stories by a writer she had mentioned in one phone call eighteen months earlier, tracked down with patient research. The card said: Still paying attention.

Year four: a silk scarf the colour of the sea not blue, not green, but the specific blue-green that the sea is in certain lights. A compass, silver, small, with N engraved on the face. A card that said: For the person who always finds her way.

She called him about the compass. "It arrived today," she said, and her voice was different. Quieter. "I cried. It's just a compass. I don't know why I cried."

"It's not just a compass."

A pause. "You sound sure of that."

"Objects carry the intent they were sent with. Whatever they meant to say, you heard it."

"Oliver," she said. Soft. Searching. The way she said his name when she was genuinely thinking.

"What?"

"Never mind." She moved on. She always moved on. "Tell me about the company."

Chapter Thirteen

The Weight of What He Saw

Four Years After Graduation October

He saw the photographs on a Wednesday.

It was late in the evening. He was in his chair with his computer open, doing nothing important scrolling through things with the partial attention of someone whose day has exhausted them. The algorithm, which had no regard for timing or mercy, offered him something.

Amelia. In a white dress, in a garden. Flowers in her hair small white ones. Her smile, which he knew every version of, in a version he hadn't seen before: composed, radiant. And beside her, a man. A man with his arm around her waist.

Engaged, the caption said. Can't believe I get to marry this woman.

He closed the app. He put the computer aside. He sat in his chair with the window dark beside him and the courtyard below empty and the lilac tree bare now, in October skeletal against the city lights, and something inside him that had been held in careful position for four years and seven months came quietly, finally, down.

Not loudly. Not with drama. Oliver didn't do loud or dramatic. It came down the way things come down when they've been held for too long.

He sat there for a long time. He thought about I believe you. He thought about a yellow cardigan and the compressed weight of a red notebook. He thought about February the corner, the cold, the moment he had not said anything. He thought about all the when that had passed.

When was gone.

He called Jack past eleven. “I’m fine,” Oliver said. “I just needed to hear someone.”

“I’m here,” Jack said.

Eventually Oliver said: “I’m going to leave. The company. The city. I’ve been thinking about New Zealand for years. I’m going.”

“You’re serious.”

“I’m always serious.”

“I’m going to transfer ownership to you. Formally. You’ve been running it better than me for two years.”

“That’s not truc.”

“It is and we both know it. You are the company, Jack. You always were. I was the idea. You are what the idea became.”

When Jack spoke his voice was different rougher than usual. "I hope it's everything you needed it to be."

"Me too," he said.

Chapter Fourteen

One More Thing

November Before He Left

He had one more thing to do before he left.

She had mentioned New Zealand once. It was years ago, a Thursday call in the second year after graduation. She'd said: If I could live anywhere. Not here. Somewhere quiet. An old house with a lot of space and no neighbours for miles and a garden. Maybe New Zealand. She'd laughed after she said it, slightly self-conscious. She had moved on immediately to something else.

He had remembered. He always remembered everything she said.

He bought a car. A Mini Cooper. Red. The colour of her notebook the red spiral-bound one from second year, the one with his attributed quote inside it. He arranged delivery through the same anonymous service.

Then he sat down to write the card. He had written many cards. This was not the same as those cards.

He stared at the blank card. He thought about four years of unsigned notes, of said and unsaid things, of objects chosen with precision and sent with care and never once claimed. He thought about what it had meant to love someone this way sideways, through chosen things.

He thought: she is getting married. She does not know that for five years from the moment she laughed across an orientation hall she has been the most present person in my life without ever knowing it.

He thought: she deserves to know. Not so that anything changes it is too late for that. But because being loved this much, this long, this carefully, was a fact about the universe. And she deserved to carry it.

He signed the card. Just his name.

Oliver.

He sealed the envelope. He completed the arrangements. He sent it.

Then he packed his bags, turned off the lights in the flat he had lived in for four years, left the lilac tree to bloom for someone else in May, and went.

PART FOUR

After the Silence

Chapter Fifteen

What the Card Said

Westbridge December

The car arrived on a Thursday, which was a coincidence that Amelia would think about later. Thursday. Always Thursday with him.

The delivery driver rang the bell of her parents' house she was staying there for the winter and she signed for something she hadn't ordered and walked out to the driveway and stood there looking at a red Mini Cooper with an actual bow on it.

"Mum," she called. Her voice came out a different pitch than intended.

Susan Clark appeared in the doorway, took in her daughter's expression, took in the car, said: "Good lord."

"There's a card."

Susan came down the porch steps. Amelia held the envelope in both hands. It was the same handwriting she had been seeing for four years clean, careful, slightly leftward in its lean. But something was different about this one. This one was heavier.

She opened it. The card was small and white and plain. It said:

You told me once that you'd like to live somewhere with no neighbours for miles and no traffic sounds. I hope wherever you end up, you find that. And I hope you get to drive there in something red.

You are one of the best things that has ever happened to me, and you didn't even know you were happening.

Happy Birthday, Amelia.

Oliver

She read it once. She read it again. She looked at the handwriting Oliver and felt something happen in her chest that she didn't immediately have a name for.

"Oliver," Susan said softly. "Oliver Hayes. The one from "

"University. Yes."

"Mum," she said. "I think I need to find him."

* * *

She went to her old room and found the box. She had always kept a box she was someone who kept things, who understood that certain objects need to be stored rather than displayed.

The shoebox under her childhood bed. She hadn't opened it in two years. She opened it now.

Four birthday cards, all unsigned until the one she was holding. A compass with N engraved on its face. A silk scarf in a colour she had never been able to name precisely sea-coloured, she always thought. A small succulent she had repotted twice. A note that said Still paying attention.

She read the cards in order. She read them again. She sat on her childhood bed, in the room where she had grown up, and counted the years.

She called Priya. "Oliver Hayes," Priya said, when Amelia had finished explaining. Not surprised. Not even slightly surprised. "I wondered."

"You wondered? When?"

"Third year. In seminar. He used to look at you it wasn't nothing."

"Why didn't you say anything?"

"Because you were living your life. And," Priya added, "because you were engaged to Marcus, Amelia."

The engagement. Marcus, who was genuinely kind, who had loved her clearly and steadily. Marcus, who was not she understood this now with a clarity that was almost physical the person she'd been privately measuring everyone against.

"I have to call Marcus," she said.

That conversation was the hardest thing she had done in years. At the end he said, "I've wondered." And then: "I think I've known for a while that you were somewhere else. That a part of you was in a room I couldn't access."

She cried. He was kinder than she deserved.

Then she called Priya back and said: "How do I find him?"

Chapter Sixteen

What Jack Said

The City Helix Solutions

She found the company first. Helix Solutions she knew the name, had heard it mentioned over the years. She took the train, walked through the city with the specific determination of someone who is doing something they know they should have done years ago.

The office was on the third floor of a glass-and-brick building. She gave her name to the receptionist and explained that she was a friend of Oliver Hayes, former partner, and needed to speak with someone who might know where he was.

"Can I help?" The voice came from behind her. She turned.

Jack Fernandez was taller than she had remembered. He was standing in the corridor with his arms crossed and an expression that was not unfriendly but was doing assessment.

"So you came," he said.

"Can we talk?" Amelia said.

"Sure. Come in."

He poured coffee without asking and led her into what had been Oliver's office she could tell from the quality of its order, the particular way the books were arranged. She looked at the single framed photograph on the desk: Oliver and Jack and another man, in front of a sign that said Helix Solutions, all three of them grinning. Oliver was grinning slightly to the left of where the camera was, which was the Oliver thing to do.

"He's gone," Jack said.

"I know. I need to find him."

Jack sat down across from her and looked at her for a moment. "I'm going to say something," he said. "And I need you to listen to it properly, because he's my person and what I'm about to help you with matters enormously to me."

"Okay."

"I've known Oliver since we were nine years old. I've watched him fall for you from the first week of university and never say a word about it. I've watched him keep every detail of every conversation you've ever had. I've watched him build a company and build a life and come home and wait, genuinely wait, because he believed" Jack stopped. He breathed. " he believed you were worth waiting for."

Amelia held her coffee with both hands. She was not going to cry. She was going to listen.

"He saw your engagement photos," Jack said. "That's when something broke. Not loudly. Something just came down, quietly, and he called me and said he was going."

"Where?"

"New Zealand."

The word landed with the specific weight of something she had said, half-embarrassed, years ago.

"He went to your dream," Jack said.

Jack reached into his desk drawer and produced a postcard. A photograph of green hills and a farmhouse, white-painted, afternoon light. On the back, in handwriting she knew: It looks exactly how she described it. I understand why she wanted it. I'm all right.

She read it twice. She set it down.

"Go get him," Jack said. His voice was rough in the way of someone feeling something they've been feeling for a long time. "He has been standing still, waiting for you, for five years. He deserves someone who runs."

Chapter Seventeen

Lotus

The Road to New Zealand

She looked at the postcard photograph. Canterbury. Green hills with a particular quality of light. She researched the region methodically, which was not how she usually did things.

A community forum for the Canterbury countryside yielded a reply within a day: sounds like the McAllister place up the valley road. New tenant moved in some months back. Quiet sort, keeps himself. Lovely fella though.

Quiet sort.

Yes. That would be Oliver.

She called her mother. Susan Clark listened to all of it the card, the compass, the years of unsigned packages, the conversation with Jack, the engagement she was ending, the plan that was forming without interrupting.

"Well," Susan said at the end. "You should go."

"I've just ended an engagement."

"I know. Go anyway."

"Amelia." Susan's voice was firm and warm at once. "Your father and I have watched you move through your life with tremendous speed and tremendous light. But we have also watched you stop, sometimes. Mid-sentence. When he texted. When he called. We noticed. We didn't say anything because it wasn't ours to say. But we noticed."

"Go," Susan said. "Take the lotus."

He had said it years ago: if anyone were ever going to make an impression on him, they should do it with a lotus. His mother's favourite flower. He liked, he had said, that it grows through murk and emerges clean.

She had remembered. She had not thought about why she had remembered at the time.

She texted Margaret Hayes. She didn't know why she texted her. She did it anyway.

Margaret replied within minutes: I was wondering when. His father says he'll drive me to the airport.

Amelia stared at this message for a long time.

Margaret added: Take care of them both. My flowers and my son.

The flight was long. She read for most of it The God of Small Things, which she had been meaning to re-read since Oliver had mentioned it at a party in December of first year. She read it now with a different quality of attention, knowing he had remembered it.

She thought about the compass. For the person who always finds her way. She thought about Oliver in a bookshop somewhere, knowing what she would want before she could articulate it. She thought about Oliver at his desk in the evenings, writing cards and not signing them.

She thought: I was loved that much. I was loved with that degree of attention and care and I didn't know.

She thought: I want the rest of my life to be knowing.

Chapter Eighteen

The Valley Road

Canterbury, New Zealand

She rented a car at the airport and drove with the windows down even though the air was unfamiliar. The Canterbury countryside had a particular quality: clean in the way that distance is clean. Grass and rain-wet earth and a sky that was bigger than English skies.

The valley road curved through a valley with hills on both sides, pale green-gold in the afternoon light, and there were sheep on the hillsides and the particular silence of places that have not been disturbed into noise. She drove slowly. She was not in a hurry now.

The farmhouse appeared after the third bend: white-painted, old, with roses along the fence line and a garden that had been tended with the particular care of someone who pays attention. She recognised the care in it.

She thought: Margaret would approve.

She parked. She sat in the car for a moment. Then she got out.

She lifted the lotus from its box with both hands. It had survived. It was open, perfectly open unfolded, clean, holding its centre with the specific dignity of a thing that grows through murk and arrives at the surface exactly as it intended to arrive.

She walked to the door. She knocked. A long pause. She knocked again.

Footsteps inside unhurried, careful, the particular footstep of someone taking a moment at the door before opening it.

The door opened.

He looked different and exactly the same. He was wearing a flannel shirt and he had paint on his right hand actual paint, dried in the particular way of oil paint and his hair was slightly longer and he had a quality of settled stillness about him that was different from the careful alertness she remembered.

He was looking at her. He was looking at the lotus.

"Amelia," he said. His voice careful. Underneath it, she could hear what he was not saying.

"Hi," she said.

A pause. "How "

"Jack. And the internet. And your postcard, which he absolutely should have told you he was going to show me."

"Oliver." She breathed. "I have an enormous number of things to say to you. I planned some of them on the flight. I've forgotten most of them because you opened the door and I'm " She stopped. She started again. "I'm sorry. That has to come first. I'm sorry for disappearing. I'm sorry for the late replies and the stopped calls."

He was very still.

"I didn't know," she said. "I genuinely didn't know. But I'm here. I came here. I carried this from London which the florist said was technically inadvisable and I came to this valley in this country, which is genuinely the most effort I have ever made in my life for anything, and I need you to know that."

He stepped forward. He took the lotus from her hands gently, with both hands, the way he handled everything he cared about. He held it for a moment. He looked at it. Then he looked at her.

"Come inside," he said. "I'll make tea."

She breathed out. The full breath. "Yes."

"You're going to have to talk to me for a long time."

"I know."

"And I'll have to talk to you too. I've been very out of practice."

Something broke open in her chest, gently, like a door being opened rather than a thing being broken. "That's okay. I'm not going anywhere."

He held the door open. She walked in.

Chapter Nineteen

The House He Built for Her

Inside The Farmhouse

The house was everything she had ever mentioned.

She understood this within minutes of being inside it, and the understanding came with a quality of feeling she had not expected not surprise, but something older than surprise, something closer to recognition. As though the house were familiar not because she had been here but because she had described it, once, to someone who had listened.

The walls were painted the colour of the sea not blue, not green, but the specific blue-green she would have chosen. The bookshelves were full, and she could see her own taste in them. His own books beside them, the spines worn in the particular way of books that have been read rather than displayed.

Plants on every surface. A succulent on the windowsill. Something flowering in a pot by the door. Everywhere, green things, tended things.

The kitchen was warm. Through the window: the garden, the hills beyond it, the afternoon light settling into gold.

"I put the lotus here," she said, setting it in a glass of water on the kitchen table. She watched it float. Clean, open, exactly as it was supposed to be.

* * *

She almost didn't notice the hallway painting at first. She noticed it on her second pass through the hallway, drawn by the size of it it was nearly as wide as the wall itself.

"Can I?" she asked.

He stood in the doorway. He looked at the cloth. He looked at her. Something in his expression was very careful. He crossed to the hallway and reached up and pulled the cloth aside.

She looked at it for a long time.

It was her. A painting oil on canvas, warm-lit, precise in the way of someone who has looked at something so carefully and for so long that they know it from the inside. She was sitting at a window, a book pressed to her chest, her face turned slightly toward the light. A library window. A specific quality of light.

Second year, she thought. The library. He had been four seats away.

"You painted this," she said.

"I learned. Over the past year." He was behind her. "I needed something to do with " He stopped.

"With what?"

"With knowing you from a distance. There was a lot of it, accumulated. It had to go somewhere."

She turned around. He was close close enough that she could see the paint dried on his hand and the care in his eyes and the five years of everything he had held quietly.

"Oliver," she said.

"I know it's a lot," he said. "I know this is "

"It's you," she said. "All of this is just you, being who you are." She looked at him really looked, with the quality of attention she should have been giving him years ago. "I should have been paying more attention."

"You paid attention," he said, gently. "You just didn't know what you were paying attention to."

She reached up and put her hands on either side of his face. She held him the way he had held the lotus with both hands, with the understanding that this was something that mattered.

"I'm paying attention now," she said.

He covered her hands with his. Paint and all.

"You're here now," he said.

"I'm here now."

Outside, the hills were going gold in the late afternoon. The lotus floated in its glass on the kitchen table, clean and open and exactly as it was supposed to be.

Inside, two people who had been taking a long time to arrive at each other finally did.

Epilogue

What They Kept

They stayed a week in the valley house before the world began to require them back. There were calls to make and arrangements to negotiate and lives in other places that needed tending. None of it was simple. They did not pretend that it was.

A week was enough for some things.

It was enough for Oliver to tell her everything he had been carrying. He did it in his way not all at once, not dramatically, but in pieces. Over meals, and over walks down the valley road in the morning, and over long evenings on the porch where the sky did extraordinary things. He told her about the orientation hall and the laugh that had changed the room. He told her about October and the succulent. He told her about the party in December, and I believe you, and what it had meant to hear his name in her voice.

She listened. Really listened, with her full self.

She told him things too. About the year she had been moving too fast to stop and feel it. About Marcus. About the first birthday package, which had made her feel known in a way that was beautiful and confusing. About reading the compass card and thinking: it was him. And then talking herself out of it.

"I'm sorry I wasn't braver sooner," he said.

"I'm sorry I wasn't more awake," she said.

These felt, for now, like enough.

* * *

Amelia kept the painting. It hung in every place they lived after that and they lived in several places, in several countries. In every flat and every house, the painting was on a wall, the girl with the book pressed to her chest in library light.

He kept the attributed quote. It sat on his desk in every office he ever had: The distrust is where the reading happens. Oliver H.

She kept the compass. She kept the scarf. She kept the succulent, which had been repotted three times by now and was approaching implausible size. She kept every card he had ever sent her, signed and unsigned alike.

* * *

They were, in the end, what they had always been to each other: two people who listened carefully and were changed by it. She had changed him first, from a distance, without knowing it. She had made him better at being in the world, more open to its warmth.

And he had loved her steadily, truly, with the particular faithfulness of someone who doesn't know how to love halfway from the first moment he heard her laugh.

Some loves live entirely in the chest of one person, quiet and unconfirmed, and are no less real for it. That is what Oliver had believed, and it had been true, and it had been enough.

But some loves given enough time, and enough lotus flowers, and a door opened in a valley in a country that smells of clean rain make it across the distance.

And that, they found, was more than enough.

That was everything.

END

A Note on the Story

This novel began with Oliver sitting in a sunlit courtyard, listening to someone's footsteps fade into the ordinary sounds of an April afternoon. It ends with a door being opened in a valley at the other side of the world. Between those two moments lies a life of quiet attention, patient love, and the particular courage of someone who expresses himself not in declarations but in objects chosen carefully and sent without his name.

Oliver Hayes is not a hero in the conventional sense. He does not overcome obstacles or achieve goals in ways that translate easily into a story of triumph. What he does is simpler and harder: he pays attention. He carries what matters. He builds things quietly and well. He waits, not passively but with the active patience of someone who understands that certain things take the time they take.

Amelia Clark is not a prize. She is a full person with a full life, who moves through the world with the generous, slightly careless warmth of someone who has never had to think very hard about connection because it has always come easily. Her blindness to Oliver is not cruelty it is simply the blindness of someone who has not been given reason to look. That she looks eventually, and comes running when she does, is not a correction of some failure. It is simply the moment when the information she needed became available.

Love radiates. It marks the people near it whether or not they are the ones feeling it. That is one of its most extraordinary qualities: you can be changed by someone else's love for someone else, simply by being near enough to see it.

Oliver never stopped giving. Not when the calls became infrequent, not when the replies came slowly, not when the engagement photographs arrived. Every birthday, something chosen. Every year, the same refusal to become someone who loved less carefully than he was capable of.

That is what this story is about, at its core: not whether love is returned, but whether love is real. Oliver's love was real. It was one of the most real things in this novel. And Amelia, when she finally understood it, understood it too.

Some people change you by being who they are. Some people love you by paying very close attention. And some stories, given enough distance and enough time and one very well-carried lotus flower, find their way home.

www.ingramcontent.com/pod-product-compliance
Ingram Content Group UK Ltd.
Pitfield, Milton Keynes, MK11 3LW, UK
UKHW021403190726
13845UKWH00028B/851

9 789357 735186